ARE ONE

MICHAEL A. CLARK

Published by Water Dragon Publishing
waterdragonpublishing.com

ISBN 978-1-962538-24-4 (Trade Paperback)

FIRST EDITION

10 9 8 7 6 5 4 3 2 1

AUTHOR'S NOTE

What if a legend walks among us, but goes unnoticed? What if a myth is reborn, but the world yawns in reply? Would the legend be slighted, the myth offended?

What if they decided it was time to let us know they were here, and ready for duty?

I started "Are One" with a bad joke: *King Arthur, Merlin and Sir Lancelot walk into a bar ...* That turned into the story that follows. I hope you enjoy it.

ARE ONE

"ORDER A LARGE HAWAIIAN, Art ... with extra pineapple. And no onions!" Drool peeked from the corners of Merle's wrinkled mouth.

"This place has lousy pizza."

"This place has big, cheap pies. I don't call that 'lousy.'"

A Bud Lite sign buzzed in the Augie's Pizza front window. Cleveland was leading the Yankees 5-3 on the TV over the men's room door. The air inside was thick with tomato sauce, oregano, and spilled beer as a light mist fell from the cool September sky.

"Merle ..."

"I'm getting hungry, Art," he rumbled.

Restraint wasn't in his Old Power vocabulary, and this modern world offered no caution to his wizened mind.

"Okay ..." I sighed.

Augie's staff labored before two massive ovens. One fellow with a pockmarked face and splotchy stubble doled sauce over a large soft crust, his arms white with flour. Another clad in a white T-shirt and soiled apron languidly tossed a disk of dough aloft three times, spreading it like a jellyfish on the incoming tide.

Merle shook his head. "Never get tired of watching them make pizzas."

He looked at me. "Never get tired of EATING them either! You ordered yet? Hawaiian, with extra pineapple! No onions!"

The decaying strip mall near where we lived harbored a tattoo parlor, a nail salon, and an urban hair braiding shop along with this dismal "Italian" greasery. I remembered enough of the Romance languages to guess that the workers here were more likely Hondurans or Syrians then from the old Papal States.

The immigrant behind the cash register scribbled on a scratch pad.

"No onions! You got that?"

The counterman nodded, once.

Three Latino girls, heavy in body and makeup, leaned over their Smartphones at a booth behind us. Four disheveled white guys were hunched over the table jammed against the dust-stained front window. One of them, clad in a denim vest with melted tattoos on his thin forearms, called out a bit too loudly, "Pile on the onions!"

Merle, engrossed in the pizza maker's craft, didn't hear. The look on his weathered face was almost beatific. "Beats shepherds' pie any day ..."

"I said PILE the ONIONS on the old man's pizza," repeated Denim Tattoo. Two of his unwashed friends snickered.

I glanced at him. Vulpine, with teeth like a Cornish hog swain. His friends looked about as fit. Was it crystal meth the kids were doing these days? People have always found new ways to degrade their bodies. Can't say I blame them.

Merle leaned on the stained wood counter; the amulet slung from his thin neck gently tapping its grimy surface. Augie's clientele would have seen an old man and his middle-aged son, both in good shape for their years. I might be in a flannel shirt and relaxed fit Levis, Merle in hospital scrubs and orthopedic shoes. The shining sword mated to my left hip would have gone unnoticed.

But then, people don't notice much these days.

"Old man wants ONIONS on his pizza!" Denim Tattoo coughed, then took a drag on his cigarette. His pals gazed at us like rodent gargoyles.

The pock-faced pizza maker tensed, as he kneaded dough over a greased pan.

I never liked the New World odor of tobacco. I've smelled far too many things burn …

Denim Tattoo jerked to his feet, stubbing out his butt in a crushed beer can.

Wasn't smoking illegal in restaurants these days?

"Onions are what that OLD man wants," he slurred. "ONIONS on his pizza!"

I swear he licked his chops.

"Onions?" Merle creaked erect at the yelping of this cur. "I *hate* onions."

No, Merle. Don't go off. Please ... God, the paperwork that would have to be forged.

My hand fell to Ex's hilt reflexively ... but I'd not unsheathe Her for this.

If I wrestled this gibbering idiot to ground quickly, his cohorts would probably run — providing Merle didn't turn them into toads. The cops (if they came) might be mollified by the staffs' telling of the big old white guy smacking around a troublesome punk.

What a crappy way to start a Friday night.

"I think old men LOVE onions on pizza. 'Cause they smell OLD!" I saw the T-square bulge in the side pocket of Denim Tattoo's green cargo pants. Goddamn right-to carry gun laws in this state ...

"Son," I said, trying to sound like Clint Eastwood. "What's your point?"

My voice used to *ring* with authority ...

"ONIONS!" snarled Denim Tattoo. Maybe this wastrel didn't know who Clint Eastwood was. I watched his toothpick fingers dangling near his concealed weapon ...

And then the door swung open and in strode The Gallant Man, clad in a pewter gray Brioni suit with a brilliant smile, wide shoulders and slim waist. Mix Cary Grant with Elvis Presley and they'd half the charisma he welded. He beamed at the restaurant's denizens. Denim Tattoo eased back on his hunches, slack jawed. I could almost hear the three Latino girls' pulse rates spike.

"Lance!" cried Merle, as he snatched the freshly boxed pizza off the counter with both hands. "What the hell are YOU doing here?"

"I guessed this fine dinery might be where I'd find you!"

The Gypsies behind the counter smiled, and the tension was gone. Who could feel like fighting, with Sir Lancelot holding court?

Damn his boasting hide.

"Hello, Art," His voice smooth, respectful. "It's been a long time."

"Yeah." Of all the pizza joints in the world, he had to pick this one. Hell, I was just getting the old man something to eat. Memories of combat and adultery were far from my mind.

Sure, they were …

Merle cradled his pizza box, and then paused by Denim Tattoo's table.

"Boo!" he said, lifting its lid.

I caught whipping shadows of clawed tentacles wriggling inside, and chitterling sounds erupting from the orifice opened via Merle's unstable magic.

Denim Tattoo blanched, his bloodshot eyes rolling back into their sockets, and hit the floor hard. His pals looked like they'd just swallowed sea urchins.

"Heh, heh … how do you like *them* onions?" Merle let the lid of the box drop and shuffled towards the door. Outside, a bright full moon was chasing away the remnants of the rain clouds.

"Old man, was that really necessary?"

"Oh lighten up, Art. The kid's still breathing. I just spooked his stunted little mind."

"You haven't lost your sense of humor, Merle," said Lance.

"Nope! And I'll reckon you haven't lost your way with the ladies either," said the old wizard. "Now what brought ya here, Lance?"

"Gwen's in trouble."

I felt that sad, addictive pull in my gut again.

"Oh?" was all I could muster.

"Gwen, huh? No shit!" said Merle, setting the pizza down on a latticed metal table frosted with bird crap. He began feasting on the contents. "Dig in, boys!" as crust and cheese flew from his mouth.

"Um, no thanks," said Lance.

"Don't let that little trick back there put ya off," said Merle. "It's good stuff! With pineapples! Art?"

"Lost my appetite."

"Suit yourself!"

A pick-up truck backfired on the main road. Moths orbited the streetlamp over Augie's front sidewalk.

Lance looked at me.

"All right," I said. "Give it to me straight. And Lance … I'd better buy it."

He nodded once and put a Gucci'd foot on the chair he'd pulled screeching from the rusting table. "Gwen's been with a high roller in the financial world. A guy with connections to some Russian oligarchs, as well as the current Chinese premier's family network. He was a bit player in the hedge game, but once Gwen hooked up with him, he took off. You know how good she is with numbers."

"Are they married?"

"Does it matter?"

"I guess not."

A moth strayed out of the streetlight's glow and got picked off by a bat.

"So, she backstopped this guy and he had some rich and powerful friends," I said. "What went wrong?"

"One of the Russian oligarchs wanted to swap Alberta tar sands oil shares to prop up some flagging Gazprom stock options. Gwen told her ... partner, that the numbers didn't add up and the profits would be eaten by transaction fees. But he didn't listen."

Merle was well into his second slice. Due to his occult prank, the pizza gave off a slight whiff of sulphur. "Goddamn world has gotten too complicated," he said, chewing. "People were better off in the old days, herding goats. Now *that's* an honest way to earn a living!"

"So this wanna-be player loses some commissions," I said. "How'd that blow back on her?"

"You know what's been happening with oil prices lately. He tried to pump his reputation back up by shorting some Falkland Islands deep-water drilling rights to the premier's cousin. The cousin wanted to meet the man he'd be dealing with, and Gwen went along. She hadn't seen the Orient since that Boxer unpleasantness a while back. The cousin took one look at Gwen, signed off on a bum deal and made a pass at her that pissed off her current paramour."

I studied my worn sneakers. A hole had opened in one, exposing my right little toe within. "And then?"

"Loud words shouted by spoiled children. The cousin was unused to being told "no". Gwen had to remind her guy pal they weren't in Kansas anymore. She calmed the situation down, something also well within her skill set."

"Nothing more futile than arguing over a woman," said Merle, waving the crust from his latest devoured pizza slice like the jawbone of an ass. "Right, boys?"

"Gwen's gotten herself out of tight spots before," I said. "What's her situation now?"

"The Chinese government has ways of incarcerating foreign 'guests' without admitting they're doing so. The guy's sweating bullets, but he's small fry. The State Department'll spring him soon. Gwen, however, is in a maximum-security medical impoundment — the old Japanese Unit 731 facility in Harbin. That charming house of horrors has been renovated by an international pharmaceutical company, at the PRC's expense."

Lance breathed deeply. "Gwen needs to get out of there, Art. Fast."

"Hmmm." Those of us Old Ones still strolling Mother Earth needed to take care when dealing with healthcare professionals. Especially those in the employ of authoritarian regimes.

Gwen, Gwen, Gwen ...

•　　•　　•

The day when we first met. Sunlit paradise of a land blessed with all the Lord could bestow, and it seemed it was there just for her and I. Dark hair and tender eyes, slim arm and sculpted jaw. Touching her hand was like stroking a silken bolt of lightning. And we leaped forward ever more passionately ...

•　　•　　•

"I've got us a direct flight out of Charlotte/Douglas to Beijing in two hours. We can connect via Cathay Air to Manchuria and be there by 9pm local time tomorrow. My intel says ..."

"We?"

"Art, I can't do this by myself. I need you ..."

"Would you, if you could?"

Merle swallowed dryly and reached for another slice.

"There's more going on," said Lance, frowning. "Since Percy suffered his … accident, I've uncovered a deep, coordinated effort by a secretive array of corporate and government interests against what's left of the Kingdom. This affair with Gwen may have been a setup."

Sir Percival had been the operations manager at a lumber mill in northern Ontario for years. His kind of work — solid and predictable. The routine of fallen timber and moist sawdust. I grieved when I heard of his death. And couldn't help thinking that if I were the ruler I used to be, he might still be with us.

God, I missed him. I missed them all.

"Accidents happen, Lance," I said.

"Not to Percy. You know how obsessive/compulsive he was. There's no *way* he'd be repairing a CNC tooling center without making absolutely sure the operating system was locked out in safety mode. A circuit snapped, blades whirled, and Percy was dead."

Lance shook his head. "Not the fate deserved for one of our best."

I rubbed my stubbled jaw. The beard kept coming in, even in this mild clime.

"The RCMP wasn't called in to investigate," Lance said. "I'm told another agency had first crack at his body."

"So that means there's some kind of conspiracy? Percy's death is linked to Gwen's getting kidnapped? Isn't that a bit of a stretch?"

But I knew Lance was on to something.

"Percy got hit, like a second-banana gangster in an old Jimmy Cagney movie," said Lance. "They wanted to take him apart," He grimaced. "To … study. I'm worried that's what they'll do to Gwen."

"Goddamn science pukes and their infernal machines!" said Merle. "Bah! Back in my day …"

"Hmmm …" I said, kicking myself for not thinking more about the circumstances surrounding Percival's passing. Christ, maybe I *was* out of the game, like Merle had said before. I looked above. The few clouds in the night sky were sharply defined. Like the crests of waves frozen before crashing on a rocky shore. So, what *have* I been doing with my life lately …?

"Percy's gone." Lance choked a little, and not for my benefit. "But Gwen's what's important now. She can outfox whatever *psychological* tests they throw at her. I doubt she's been harmed … yet." He pursed his lips. "But medical testing methodology is improving, and … I think they may be after our Big Secret."

"Immortality," snorted Merle. "Ya ask me, it's highly overrated." But the old mage looked weary and sad. As if wondering how much richer life might have been if his monstrous magic would have allowed him to pass it naturally.

The three of us stood around the outdoor table, eyes cast away from each other.

After all this time … were we *ashamed* of this dreaded gift?

An owl hooted in the night breeze, beyond the strip mall lights. I drew some comfort from the primal sound.

"So, tell me who 'they' are again?" I asked.

"I don't know who's behind it, Art." said Lance, glancing at Merle. The old man was hunched over, oblivious. "But I do know they're serious."

"What are 'we' going to do once we get to China?" Gwen trapped by a powerful cabal in a 21st century house of Frankenstein was a problem.

Ex hung patiently at my side. I gently laid my hand on Her hilt.

Every problem has a solution. Doesn't it?

"It'll have to be a quick extraction, from a heavily guarded installation," said Lance. "I'll be able to get us close enough to breach *most* of the security systems. But not all of them may be … electro/mechanical in nature."

"You want Merle to deal with whatever ancient Chinese secrets may be holding Gwen prisoner." I said, nodding to our old sorcerer still lost in thought. "What do you want *me* to do?"

"To do what you've always been best at, Art."

A sprinkler went off several yards away, feebly watering the dried patch of soil at the base of a dwarf sugar maple. It hadn't rained much in the past six months. The land here was dry, slumping. Unwell.

Like I'd felt, for so long. I used to be strong, confident, and virile. Making the right decisions in war and peace.

And the land prospered …

"Can you do anything from here, old man?" God, asking Merle to hurl an incantation from this distance was the dice. But I had to use all the tools available to solve the problem. Like I used to do …

"If I were still a young buck like you," the wizard straightened a bit. "Could make the boughs break with a snap of my finger." Fallen leaves from the few remaining trees around the parking lot swarmed and flowed like a thin blanket of ochre and sand in a sudden wind. "I'll need to be close. Wanna make sure I'm ... Damn it, Art! My mind keeps wandering!" He shook his head. "I used to be ... *focused*!"

"I know," I said, not knowing what else to say.

Merle was fading. From immense heights but fading. For all his faults ... what would we do without him? Lance looked away, off into the chill night sky.

"But," Merle said. "It's good you're thinking like a leader again, son."

Assuming we could breach the defenses surrounded Gwen's holding area, and that Merle could unleash his magic at the right moment ... Yeah. It would probably mean chest wheezing and scuffing over rough ground and dodging searchlights, just to get close enough ... Like a raid on a Saxon camp, back in the old days.

Lance drew in a breath and looked me in the eye.

"Our Queen needs her King," he said.

And without a hint of pretense my dearest friend and the thief of my love bent to one knee. "And so do I, your most faithful servant."

I felt a bursting pride in that honest gesture, and the ancient thrill of responsible power. For this moment, before my finest knight and our grandest wizard, I *was* a king again. Respected for all the right reasons. To hold onto that moment, that it might last an eternity ...

But the sounds of the modern world around us, cars and the tinfoil buzzing of a cellphone.

This time wasn't *our* time. But it would have to do.

"Then our Queen awaits us," I said, squaring my shoulders. "And we should not tarry to be at her disposal."

Merle dabbed a tear from his weathered face with a tomato-stained napkin, then blew his nose in it. "Boys, you don't know how long I've been waiting for you two to get together again. You better get me stoned," he sniffed. "I don't fly good on airplanes these days."

•   •   •

Lance drove us to the airport in his Aston Martin DB11. He'd offered two Xanax to Merle before we passed through security, but the old man had grabbed the bottle of pills from his hand and emptied its contents in a single gulp.

"*That* should do it!" Merle said. By the time we were seated, Camelot's magician was snoring, head resting against the cold starboard window.

"He looks peaceful," said Lance. We were in the pair of First Class seats behind the old mage, Lance having bought the aisle seat next to Merle to keep it open. A bit of turbulence, normal when curving down over the Aleutians, jostled the 737-Max. I was on my third scotch. Not bad booze, for a commercial flight.

"Yeah. When he's passed out."

"How is he, Art? He seems to be ... drifting."

"There's days when he's still sharp," I said, nipping at the tiny bottle. "But those days are getting farther apart. He'll go off on a rage, or get confused ..." I shifted in my seat. Ex in her scabbard fit comfortably in the tight space, as she always did.

"We were at Target the other day, and he saw a mirror in the home furnishings department. It was just a cheap mirror ... from Mexico or someplace. But Merle went off, and the microwave popcorn started crackling three isles over," I shook my head. "Then the fake fireplace logs, those ones made out of sawdust and paraffin, ignited in the home goods section. 'Goddamn Morgan and her filth hole!' he'd shouted at the mirror, as the store's sprinklers rained down on a stinging fog. 'That bitch can't have her way with meeeeeee … '"

"How'd you talk yourselves out of that?"

The prettiest flight attendant of the crew brought Lance another glass of Bordeaux. He smiled just enough to spark her fantasies in return.

"I grabbed him and made for the exit. Damn it, I really needed to get some dental floss. And they had three packs on sale for $7.99."

Lance sipped his fresh glass of wine. "Well, *that* was a loss."

I made a fist with my aged right hand. It hurt. Like it has for a long while.

"Sometimes Merle says I'm shirking my destiny … that I need to get 'back in the game'." I recrossed my legs, to work out the inflight stiffness. "I don't know what the hell he's talking about."

"I think he knows."

I looked at Lance, then out the window at the distant land passing far below. I couldn't have conceived of this when I was a boy, herding sheep and skipping stones across the lake. Before Merle and Ex changed my life. Now, hurtling through the sky was just a matter of frequent flyer miles and forged passports.

Mother Earth. When did I start finding you so trivial?

"Maybe Merle has a point, Art," continued Lance. "Things have always been dicey, what with famine and wars and now Facebook and COVID. People feel that they're rudderless, adrift. And that the land is being wasted for no good." He settled back in his seat. "They're angry and afraid, and don't know what to be angry and afraid about. This crap with Gwen ... It's only the tip of the iceberg."

"So 'They' are on to us, after all this time?" I tried sounding sarcastic.

Lance pulled an iPad from the in-flight pouch at his knees and called up a series of flow charts and email chains. "This is what I know," he said, flipping across the flat thin screen as adept as a 14-year-old searching for manga porn. I digested the data as quickly as I could, emptying my dwarf bottle of Scotch.

"Hmmm ..." Spiders started crawling across my brain.

"And this is where I think it's going." Lance stabbed his finger at the thin vibrant screen, an interactive map labeled with tiny pentagrams.

"Nice graphics," I said. "Those little stars mean ...?"

"Bad tidings for the Table." Lance frowned.

The cute flight attendant leaned over Lance to ask if I wanted another drink. I nodded, gambling I'd be sober by show time.

Lance lightly stroked the edge of his portable flat screen. "And now, Gwen ..."

The pensive cast on his face spoke volumes. I almost felt sorry for him.

And then, for the millionth time, I remembered.

My best friend and my wife. Together.

The plane's superstructure creaked in the high frozen air.

"So, if all this is true, what do you want *me* to do?" Another bump of turbulence and Merle stirred slightly his seat before returning to his slumber.

"WE want you to do what you've always done best," Lance said respectfully, as if beckoning me towards the solution to a puzzle he already knew. "I've seen many things in this world, Art."

"Yeah? So have I."

"So, do you remember, 'the Land and the King are one'?

"I remember the line, Lance. I've seen the old movies." And I had. Christ, Robert Goulet ...

"Hollywood never got us right," said Lance, regarding his glass of wine. "And that's not a bad thing. But *we* remember when magic wasn't confined to a doddering old vagrant and a man wearing an invisible sword."

"You'll be making your point sometime before we land, I hope?"

"Men still want a king who'll stand for right," Lance said, his voice deepening. "They need to know that justice has a name and a face, and a strong right arm to back it up."

"Really? Look at that bloated orange clown they had elected back there." I jerked my thumb to the east, over the tailing end of the New World. "Some thirst for principled leadership from the masses."

"Blobs like that can only huckster the mob for a short while, Art. *Real* devotion can only be justified by a worthy leader."

"Yeah."

"You know that's the way we felt about *you*, my king. You know that we all trusted you. With our hearts, and our lives."

•   •   •

God, were we a force to be reckoned with. Me at the lead, with Lance and Percy and the rest. Sword and shield, hooves over fields. We took casualties, but persevered. And we could feel good at the end of the day after riding to the defense of the oppressed.

Or so I always told myself.

It wasn't that simple, that clear. Mistakes were made. I made them. Innocents died.

And I had many sleepless nights ...

•　　　•　　　•

"We weren't perfect, Lance," I said, hankering for that next mini bottle of Scotch. "Just Middle Age barbarians in the romantic haze of a myriad mis-transcribed stories."

"That's all you think we were?" said Lance, with a rakish smirk. "Entertainment fodder for cartoons and Broadway musicals? You know that's bullshit. Trust me, Art. There are powerful forces that understand we were a *whole* lot more than that."

"So?"

"So, they're afraid of us. Maybe ..." his handsome profile sagged. "I don't blame them."

Lance's flight attendant admirer presented me with a new drink. I nodded in a polite, confident way, as the well-dressed business traveler I appeared to her would.

"Those of us left from the old days *are* a threat, Art. To them, if you think about it. People fear what they don't understand," said Lance. "And they're jealous when they can't get what they think others might have."

There were many issues raising their heads over our little reunion. And these issues would need to be dealt with. One at a time.

"Well," I said, figuring that I'd better start playing the role of field marshal if that's what my old friend had planned for me. "Then isn't it about time to start planning this mission?" I emptied half the bottle of Scotch. "If I'm going to be riding to my ex-wife's rescue, I'd like to get more information on what I'll be riding *into*."

Lance smiled. "Aye, my lord."

We huddled over his iPad until the cabin lights flickered for the descent into Chinese airspace, forging ideas for a campaign like we had so many times before. Merle snored the whole way through.

•   •   •

Our connection from Beijing to Harbin on Air China was late, but Lance had factored that into our schedule. He texted on a cellphone definitely *not* purchased at a suburban mall kiosk while we sat in the terminal's smoky private VIP lounge bar.

Merle was nursing a double of Stoli's vodka while watching the Cavs playing the Lakers halfway around the world, his shoulders square and his eyes clear. He seemed more ... himself since we landed.

"Don't fret about me, son," Merle said, gently swirling a rind of lemon around the lip of his drink. "I'll deal with what needs to be done."

I nodded, hoping he was right. Steely Dan played softly over the bar's sound system. Around us, the soured cream of the international business elite buzzed and murmured. Lebron James dunked hard, and two Swedish salesmen drinking martinis across the bar cheered. They'd have seen us as a pair of fit executives traveling with our company's venerable owner.

Lance set his phone down on the bar. "I've confirmed the arrangements," he said.

"With whom?"

"Some who work for money — which I generously provide." Lance took a swig from the glass of absinthe resting on its coaster of harlequin paperboard.

Never got what Hemingway and Allister Crowley saw in the drink. Tasted like castor oil to me.

"Others … who've kept faith in what we once were. They know the trumpeted call to rise for the sake of the oppressed will be sounding once more. They've vowed to answer it."

L.A. continued pummeling the Cavs, to the merriment of the Swedes. "LeBron is the MAN!" one of them exclaimed.

"You didn't used to be so … ideological, Lance," I finished my neat glass of GlenDronach. At least I'd have one last top-shelf Scotch.

"I didn't used to be a lot of things," he replied. "I didn't understand what we really meant to people over the years."

The absinthe was going down bitter, I could tell.

"I didn't realize the gift … and the responsibility we wasted. Maybe I was waiting for you to tell me." He shook his head when the bartender asked if he wanted another. "But you never did, Art."

Merle took a bite from the cheese plate arrayed before us.

"This trip might settle an old score, boys," he said. "Maybe not the one you're thinking of right now." The old man looked sharper than he had in ages. There was strength in him again.

Thank God.

Lance's phone buzzed once, vibrating on the lacquered marble bar top. He glanced down and said, "It's time."

"I reckon so," I said, lying to myself that I wanted to go through with this.

"Getting to Gwen will be the easy part," said Merle. "I'll handle that." He passed the citrus skin one last time around his glass, and then drained it of vodka. "You'll have enough to deal with, after."

•　　•　　•

A Porsche Cayenne GTS was waiting for us in the airport's rental parking lot. Merle sat cross-legged on the fine leather upholstery in the back next to the black duffle bag that I figured held Lance's tools of the trade. The Harbin night sky was ablaze with neon lights. Mammoth work cranes attended skyscrapers under construction like giant, skeletal insects. The main thoroughfare was as clogged with traffic at 11pm as an Atlanta rush hour. Hydrocarbon fumes thickened the cold damp air.

"We're about a quarter mile out from where we'll deploy," said Lance, turning left onto a side street flanked by a KFC and a Starbucks.

I'd rescued Gwen from peril before. But *this* was as far removed from our medieval past as was the dark side of the moon. Our plan relied on stealth, speed and the magics that the mystic mage of Camelot would hopefully be able to summon one more time. Like a father taking his young son's hand while crossing a road, I grasped Ex's hilt.

And not for the first time wondered who the parent was, and who the child.

Apartment buildings already slumping due to poorly enforced construction codes lined the road, their sparsely-lit windows like gaping teeth. Lance swerved around an open manhole and just missed hitting a guy riding a moped without lights.

"Jesus!" he said. "Don't they have streetlights around here?"

Lance was tense. And Lance was *never* tense.

"Ease off the gas a bit, son," said Merle.

I glanced back at the old wizard. He calmly stroked his amulet. "There's a Web of Announcement hanging over the next right turn. Go through not too fast, nor too slow. We don't want to give ourselves away just yet."

"Web Of ..."

"Static magic, Art, from around the time of the early Chin Dynasty. Supposed to give adepts warning of oncoming foes. Simple spells, sort of the equivalent of the home security systems they sell on TV these days." Merle pulled on his left ear, twice, and I remembered that meant something.

"You might want to cut the lights, Lance," he said.

"Okay."

The crappy apartments had given way to a business park that could have sat off an interstate outside Toledo or Jacksonville. Single story brick and glass offices with Chinese signage and smaller English text below, but no curb cuts for handicapped access. A Volvo SUV was parked in front of building 731. One dim light shone from a shuttered window.

"Here?" Lance asked.

"Yes," said Merle. "Next to that tree and kill the engine."

"Didn't you say this used to be a concentration camp?" I asked.

"Facilities for medical experiments run by the Japanese before and during WWII, testing germ warfare and vivisection techniques on POWs and civilians," said Lance. "After the war, the 'doctors' running the place got immunity from U.S. officials who were afraid they'd take their carefully accumulated knowledge of war crimes behind the Iron Curtain. Since then. much of the installation's been razed. Part of it's still there, though. Underground. But still in use."

"People will always bully and torment," said Merle. "Be on your toes, boys."

We got out.

Wet leaves clogged the storm drain at our feet, smelling faintly of motor oil and stubbed cigarette butts.

That sense I got before battle arose. Nauseous fear bubbling, and then ...

I'd not felt this way in a very long time.

"Lance, see if one of your toys will deal with the electronic security system," said Merle. "I'll attend to what magics await us."

Lance clicked a utility belt bearing a silenced Glock and other tools around his waist and pulled a sleek instrument from his black satchel.

"Are you good with this?" I asked him.

"Too late not to be." Lance smiled. "It's been awhile, hasn't it?"

"Yeah." I smiled back.

"Lance ..."

"Sorry, Merle." Lance activated his device, muted blue LEDs glowing. He made several practiced adjustments.

"High end, but pretty standard stuff, probably L3 circuitry running SAIC license software. Give me a second ..."

An owl hooted, breaking the distant sounds of the city.

Merle strode towards the front door of the office building, an office building like anywhere in the corporate world. He cocked his head at the logo stained in glass and circled a slim finger once before him.

"Voodoo?" He chuckled, and then spoke a word long and without vowels.

"This is a setup," I said.

"We kicked that around back on the plane, Art," said Lance, still engrossed in his tool.

"Yeah, but I didn't think it would be so ... obvious." Ex hummed by my side, patiently waiting to see the light again. So we'd make it through, one more time.

The door lock clicked, and Lance said "We're in."

"Let's go, boys," said Merle, as I opened the door for him.

Lance followed, as did I.

It was a standard open reception area, two couches and a glass table topped with an ashtray and several magazines by the far wall. The front desk was stained wood, with a dark flat screen hovering above. High ceiling, potted plants, institutional baize carpet ending in black and white checkered tile leading to the dark corridor within. The same as an office in Stockholm, Johannesburg, or San Mateo might be. Stunted streetlight peered in through slatted windows, just enough to see faint shadows.

"Incoming," Merle announced.

There were five of them, and I had time to kick myself for not checking out potential ambush spots before they were on us. Two popped up on my right from behind an array of file cabinets, and Ex slid out of her sheath like cold mountain runoff in the new spring.

Gwen had once said that I welded Excalibur like she was a part of my arm.

No, darling, I'd replied. I was HER arm.

One guy had an Uzi with a silencer, the other a poor copy of a Shinto era Katana samurai sword. Ex cleaved the Uzi in two and then I swung left and slashed down through the wrist of Mr. Shinto. He gasped, and I slammed Ex's butt end into his jaw. Mr. Shinto went down, and I turned to Mr. Uzi, who was staring dumbfounded at his emasculated weapon. A little slow for pro assassins, I thought, as Ex ripped through his thigh with the course, clinging sound sharp steel makes through living meat.

God help me, I've missed this.

Lance laid one of his attackers low with a hard kick to the knee, then rolled away, pistol drawn as the other flailed at him with a pair of nunchakus. Lance fired once, hitting his assailant in the right shoulder. Four down ...

But *we* weren't the target.

Hired goon #5 crouched ten feet from Merle, and three Shuriken flew from his right hand like buttered wasps.

Merle cocked his head casually ... and the sharp-edged disks gently tumbled to the floor before him like spare change dropped into a beggar's bowl.

"I don't like those things," he said, fixing his black-clad attacker with a preternatural stare. "And I'll know who bade you greet us with such ... alacrity."

The assassin froze like an enthralled rabbit.

"No," said Merle. "The gold they say they'll pay won't balm your soul."

The ninja collapsed in a heap at Merle's iron glare.

He was all the way back. Merlin, Master of Magic again.

"Sad pathetic pawns of power," he sighed. "Time's a-wasting. Shall we?"

I willed my pounding heart back into my chest and took the lead, with Merle close behind and Lance guarding the rear. I felt a little gratified that Lance was breathing as hard as I was.

"Down the hall. The staircase on the left," said Merle.

"Your 'arrangements' didn't warn you about our welcoming committee?" I wheezed.

"Sorry," replied Lance. "When we get out of this, I'll file a lawsuit."

"Do that. Did you get anything out of the guy before he fainted, Merle?"

"Murky thoughts. His father never told him he loved him. There was something darkly familiar holding back his mind," said the wizard. "If I had more time ... But we'll find out soon enough. Oh, nice work back there, men. You haven't lost a step."

Both of us smiled at Merle's complement.

"Hold up." The mage raised his right hand before the staircase door, next to a framed inspirational poster of a submerging whale's tail. "Toltec death-shroud. Strong, but needs recasting."

"Maybe there's been a budget cutback in their magical maintenance department," said Lance, still breathing heavily.

"Hush, Lancelot. The ante's been upped." Merle tugged his left ear twice and murmured something that sounded like, "Yaztremskilonborgconigliaro," and the door shimmered like soapy water filming off a car window, solidifying after the old man turned its knob.

"What was that?" I asked.

"Backwards Sanskrit," he said. "A go-to spell for opening skewered doors of perception." Merle pondered the flight of stairs revealed below, dimly lit by safety lamps. "Follow me. I doubt we'll have any surprises before we get to the bottom."

Lance and I followed, our footfalls faintly echoing on cast cement. The walls around us weighed in like a cold cloak.

I wondered who Gwen might turn to first … and how this wasn't the time or place to worry about shit like that. God, how we never really grow up.

Then I thought of a quest, long ago.

•　　　•　　　•

Some frightened herdsmen from a distant corner of the realm claimed a dragon was ravaging their flocks, producing charred sheep bones as evidence. The monster's lair was deep below a knoll far beyond a putrid moor, and they were sore afraid to face the menace themselves.

I could have passed this off onto another knight of the Table. Dragon-slaying was a young man's job, right? But, perhaps chaffing at the bonds that leadership was already clamping on me, I girdled myself up and traveled to this far part of the land, crossing a stinking bog to the cave's mouth below which this alleged destroyer of ungulates resided.

I hunched into the cavern, Ex at Her ready. Down I went, casting dangling roots and cobwebs aside, until the strong scent of sulphur rang in my nose.

Strange luminescence lit the small chamber before me, sparkling cinders of rose, mauve and blue. And before me, curled on a bed of peat moss lay the dragon, breathing slowly. Not so fearsome a beast. Perhaps as tall as a stallion, but thin as a whippet. A black forked tongue flicked to the rhythm of her ancient heartbeat, and then she lifted her armored head towards me, yellow eyes both alien and forgiving.

Ex returned to Her scabbard, and I knelt before this last of wondrous dragon kind. Her dark tongue tasted me, and horny nostrils prodded my outstretched hand. I smiled, stroking the brittle scales along her snout, as I would my favorite hound. The dragon sighed with a sound that almost said, "Finally." And then she was gone.

I wept, arranged a stone for her pillow, leaving her as comfortable as I could.

•   •   •

After a short eternity, we arrived at a landing with an encaged red-light bulb casting its dim pallor over us. A horizontal latch barred the staircase access door, like a hundred Hampton Inns in which I'd stayed before. A placard in Japanese, yellow with age, hung to the left.

"May you humbly forget what Duty asks you to witness," translated Lance. He was always good with languages.

Merle rolled his shoulders and said "Pymatuning. Mahoning. Neshannock." Something snapped like a pea pod, as the door gave a subtle metallic sigh.

"Mother Earth, guide your children in what will come."

That was the closest Merle ever said to a prayer.

Lance started forward, but I shook my head.

"*My* wife, remember?" I whispered, raising my left hand and fingers one, two, three ... then I kicked the hotel door open hard, and rolled to my right, as Lance spun to the left, pistol ready. Like we've done so many times before.

The room before us was softly lit, mauve and amber walls in a high ceiling layout, like a million-dollar condo overlooking New York's Lower West Side. Track lights, plush carpet, and a granite topped island counter by the kitchenette on the left, topped with a rack of designer olive oils. Tea was brewing, and a bouquet of tulips lay arranged beneath a portrait of Oscar Wilde.

This wasn't what I expected from an abandoned gas chamber.

Lance's eyes darted around the space, as Merle entered. The amulet around his neck flashed prismatic hues.

On a white couch before a gas lit fireplace stirred a figure, shaking off a finely knitted afghan blanket. I so knew how that body arose from slumber, slim limbs elegantly lifting her up, like a lotus gently turning toward the sun.

"Merle? Lance ..." And then our eyes locked. "Art!"

With greyhound speed she bolted from the couch and into my arms. How such a thin woman could crush my ribcage, I don't know. I just reveled in the scent of her dark hair, and the heart beating in rhythm with mine.

Oh, damn the consequences ... this was worth it all.

"You big dumb ape, you shouldn't have come here ..." she said into my chest. "You don't know ..."

"Oh, but he's about to find out," said a voice etched in shadow and cured with brine.

The fake fireplace flickered, as did the lights above. A shape formed, as the stench of a funeral pyre filled my nostrils.

"The bitch is back," stated Merle.

And there she was, in all her hideous beauty. Grace Kelly with fangs, a hunchbacked Marilyn Monroe, Sophia Loren riddled by smallpox. Medusa, Lilith, Circe — all in one package.

"Well, the once and stupid king has arrived! And you've brought Lover Boy and my favorite Useless Old Man! Come to save this sweet, innocent damsel in distress?"

"Morgan," I said, my throat dry as the Gobi Desert.

"I could congratulate you three stooges on getting this far into our bungalow," she replied. "But since I arranged it all, I won't."

"What have you done to her?" said Lance, crouched in his combat firing position.

"Surprisingly little, Boy-toy. Your trollop and I here have been getting reacquainted. Just two girlfriends kicking over old times." I felt Gwen's jaw tighten as the abomination slinked slowly around the couch toward us, designer gown trailing against the fine upholstery. "You're not *that* stupid to think pulling the trigger will do any good. Are you, Romeo?"

"Humor me, "said Lance, steadying his aim. "Maybe I've loaded silver bullets."

"Art." Gwen murmured. "She's worse than ever ..."

"What do you want, crone?" asked Merle, his white hair gently tossed by the ceiling fan. "If you still have a beef with me, we can settle it. Let them be. You've tormented them enough."

"No I haven't, Dinosaur. But *we* will settle accounts. That I promise."

Ex felt oddly heavy in my hand.

Gwen shivered and then faced her jailer, squaring her perfect jaw.

"You've promised to break us for centuries, Morgan," she said. "But we're still here. One might think you're more bark than bite these days"

My wife, feisty as ever.

Merle's ancient face crinkled with the hint of a smile. "Ceemagonia, ceetunguska, Ceeceeroswell," he intoned.

"Merlin ..." Morgan tilted her head, awful profile cutting the artificial light.

"D.Boon, DD.Ramone, D. Ukesnider ..."

"Shriveled old raisin, your 'Earth' magic is like a Pinto to my Porsche."

"Diplodocus, Triceratops, all that resides thus ..."

"You're boring me, codger ..." Morgan gritted her unnaturally white teeth.

Morgan was powerful, Merle had said long ago, but not omnipotent. She'd plagued my kingdom for eons ...

When was the last time I'd thought about "my kingdom"?

Christ, not two days ago I was just getting Merle a fucking pizza. My whole world had been taking care of him, while keeping my own thoughts numbed with alcohol. But Merle hadn't needed *me* all these years, I just realized.

I ... needed him.

"Let justice be untrussed, and life for all redone!" Camelot's sorcerer hadn't spoken with such power in ages.

Creaking sounds, like mammoth gears crunching ancient rust between pitted teeth, and the scent of pine sap burning. A dank halo of pus wove around Morgan, casting sickly shadows through the dim lit room.

Merle made the sign of the pentagram; a symbol so long misunderstood and then uttered, "Bytor gaylesayors!"

Morgan winced, then growled, "You were promising for a shaved ape, Merlin. You had the seed of power, even as a drooling youth. I had hopes for you and your urchins."

"No, hag," said Merle. He clasped his wrinkled hands strongly together. "You hoped for pain and enslavement. And that's why I spurned you."

"*You* spurned ..." Morgan shimmered like coal light through stale beer. "Talk about alternative facts. You could have joined me in ruling this mud ball, senile one. *You* walked away, to dwell with these ... creatures."

"Nay, harlot." Merle said, furrowing his brow.

Morgan leaned over the sofa, striking a swimsuit model pose. "Isn't that what you really wanted, Merle? A grand stage on which to perform your petty magics?" She gestured towards us with a snake-ish finger. "You led these slacker punks here to believe there was a 'higher cause' to what you were doing. I'll grant you; they are gullible ..."

"If we're so feeble," asked Gwen. "Why waste your magnificence on us? Are we a scab you can't keep picking at? Or do you *need* us more than you like to admit?"

Lance and I exchanged glances. My wife might easily get us all killed.

"Slut, you make a good point every now and then." Morgan rose from her pose off the couch, flushing ebony maggots from her body. "You always were smarter than these two semi-eunuchs. Never understood what you saw in either of them."

"Fuck you," Lance said.

"Oh, I've done all of you at one time or another," said Morgan. "You were the lamest beef, Don Juan. I should have gotten a Tony for the faking I did with *you*."

"Ewwwww ..." Lance's face twisted.

Ex by my side, was feeling ... wrong. Everything was feeling wrong.

Merle breathed deeply, as if gathering himself for a final push up a steep hill.

"Moeberg, Sanfordbraun ..."

"Shut up, old man! I've power that dwarfed yours when you were young and virile!"

"Old I may be ... but not the fool I was before, Morgan. I can see you clearly now."

"The reign is gone? I congratulate your optometrist, gnome. But I'm ascendant now, and this world *will* be mine. Finally." Morgan's nails trailed across the granite kitchen counter, ringing through my bones. "In a blink of my eye, humans grew from nomads to nuclear weapons. Impressive, in a way ... But they're still troglodytes, ignorant of the knowledge that might set them free. And I like that."

She shook her head, luxurious cobwebs of hair billowing.

"Faith!" She laughed. "Faith is what the toddlers ruling this diseased realm offer. Faith and submission. Well, *I'll* give them something to have faith in ..."

"You're not taking The Land," I said.

A crocodile smile slashed Morgan's mouth. "Oh no, hero?"

I could barely keep from retching in her presence.

"You Bland-tastic Four were the last that might have stopped me," Morgan said. "All it took was money to arrange this little reunion. Mortals are so fucking cheap," she snorted. "Two million rubles here, five million euros there, and they'll gleefully sell out family, friendship, and country. So richly deserving of the obedience I'll demand from them."

"Your plan ends here, wench," said Merle, tugging once, then again on his earlobe. "Olivatony, Brocklou. Perrygaylord be done with you."

"Damn you, old man ..." Morgan shuddered, as a myriad of blazing pixels bound around her like Saturn's rings. "A parody of yourself in valor ..."

"You have to *pronounce* your spells now, barren one," Merle said through gritted teeth. "You have to *focus*, since you're aping our 'form'. You pathetic shadow of a fertile past ..."

Morgan ... sighed, age draining power from her hideously beautiful face.

"Move, Lance!" shouted Gwen. Seeing an opening, she spun away from me like a martial arts ballerina, delivering her right foot straight into the she-monster's stomach.

"You fucking cunt ..." Morgan blurred a bit, like ink oozing along freshly drawn comic strip lines. She reared back, slashing away Merle's ensnarling rainbow curtain. "Damn you all!"

Gwen hit the floor, hard.

Ex tingled in my hand. Yes, please ...

"For my Queen and King!" Lance's pistol slammed shots home, hot empty casings bouncing on the plush floor. Morgan shrieked, and an impossibly long arm flung my bravest of knights against the kitchen's granite island. Lance wouldn't walk away from this fight.

Enraged, Morgan hurled a crimson lightning bolt at Merle, who deflected it into pearl raindrops. Ozone crackled in the sterile air, and I could almost hear the old man's knees buckle against Morgan's ethereal power.

God, this is happening too fast.

"Illigitemus Bernie Carbo est," wheezed Merle, and a thicket of thorned bamboo enveloped our foe. "Swing away, boy," he croaked, sweat pouring from his weathered face. "When you see your pitch … Swing away!"

Ex lightened. Familiar, part of me again …

The ethereal forest around the monster splintered into obsidian shards, as Morgan erupted, bellowing, "The end of you, old man!" She raised her awful hands, electricity crackling like a Jacob's ladder in an old Boris Karloff film from her fingers.

Morgan couldn't defeat Merle while dealing with the rest of us, I realized. One of us might get a good shot. And that one left was me.

Ex leapt into my hands as I strode forth, like Willie Stargell taking a Jerry Koosman fastball over the right field wall in old Forbes Field. Too late, Morgan saw my uppercutting swing. Ex slid clean through her neck, and Morgan's astonished face didn't hit the floor before she was gone, a black hole sucking shattered cinders into the void.

And all went blessedly dark.

•   •   •

I was dreaming of a day, long ago. When thin clouds of sea foam laced the late summer sky, and the warm air was full of ripening grain and sweet flowers. I'd ridden to a hill overlooking a small stream that gently wove 'round stands of beech and clumps of cattails. It was my favorite place for doing nothing.

Only Merle might ever come this way. Which he did, on this particular day.

He wasn't so old then, but old enough. He'd been keeping his powerful magics at bay for a time, choosing to deal with the world's troubles the way the rest of us did. Merle had a hefty goatskin of fortified wine with him (as usual), and we reclined in the shade of a large oak, my horse grazing contentedly in a patch of clover nearby. The clouds stretched like spider webs against azure blue, and Britain was never so peaceful and glorious.

Merle told me of things that would come, spinning tales of industrious men weaving iron and stone pillars out of the earth. Of horseless tracks carrying people to and fro at gale speed, and devices both large and small that were wonders to compete with his wizardry.

It was a lazy day, and I had no commitments. So I listened and dozed off. And awoke to find the old mage had gone, and shadows were creeping across the land.

•　　　•　　　•

My eyelids opened and I was in bed. Ex by my side, of course.

Gwen was leaning over me. "Welcome back, my king," she said.

"Where ..."?

"UPMC/Hamot Medical Outpatient Center in Erie, Pennsylvania." Gwen rested back in her chair. "It's a community walk-in clinic. As safe and quiet as can be.

You're being treated for dehydration and stress due to overwork. A fairly accurate diagnosis."

I rested my chin on my chest, aware of the tube in me, and the wires linked to an array of machines. Memory started oozing back. "Lance ..."

"The doctors say he'll be walking again in a week or two. You know how resilient he is. From what I could gather passing by the nurses' station, he's managed to have gone down on a couple of them already in his short time here."

I smiled.

"He asks about you." Gwen pursed her lips. "This isn't the way I would have wanted you two to mend your ties. But I'm glad it has."

"So am I."

A dove cooed outside the window.

"Looks like he was right about a conspiracy against us old folks," I said. "Should have suspected that Morgan was behind it all." I'd be having nightmares about what had happened for weeks to come. But if Morgan were truly banished ... "Oh, nice takedown on her back there."

"*You* taught me that move, remember?" Gwen said with a dimpled smile.

"Yeah, I remember. Merle ...?"

Gwen looked away. There was the faint screech of a cart in the hall outside, and a muffled call for an attendant to Room 714.

"It was Merle who brought us here ... You collapsed, after killing that damn witch." Gwen wiped away a tear. "I was crawling towards you. Merle turned translucent, like the wings of a dragonfly. He looked down at me with milky eyes and whispered, 'Remember, daughter.

The land and the king ...' He waited a beat, and I knew what he need to hear. So I said, 'Are one.'"

"Then his amulet flashed ochre and amethyst, and Merle just ... went away." She erupted in sobs, long dark hair cascading down on my forearm.

I cupped my hand trailing medical tubes over hers. How wrinkled they were, our hands like river deltas after a spring flood.

"I *knew* he'd have an escape plan," Gwen said after a few minutes. "He always did. Before blacking out, I thought of *here*. And here's where we are."

"So ..." I asked. "What now?"

"What now?" Gwen gazed towards the window; blinds pulled up to let in the sunshine. Thankfully, the mammoth TV hanging from the ceiling was silent. A Styrofoam cup half full of purple Jell-O rested on the metal tray on my left. My stomach growled. At least *that* part of me was still working.

"Well." She sat back in her chair. "I've accumulated some wealth over the years. We could lay low, open a bed and breakfast place down around Conneaut Lake and watch the world go by."

"We?"

"Or ... Britain's Prime Minister has called a snap election two months hence. Cardiff West's MP won't be defending his seat due to a desire to spend more time with his family sparked by the exposure of some embarrassing sexual improprieties." Gwen leaned back towards me. "I have property in that part of Wales."

"And ...?"

"I've seen the arrogance and depredations of the elites over the years, Art." she said. "The people want calm, justice and stability in the land ..."

"What does this have to do with ...?"

"I've connections. There's an organization in place. You can run for Parliament as an outsider vowing to drain the swamp of entitled interests ..."

"You gotta be fucking kidding me. I'm NOT a ..."

"You're a leader. And the Land has had precious few of those recently."

"Gwen, I don't know shit about Brisk-it ..."

"Brexit, and I do. You'll learn quickly ... as you always have. The people will see in you what they want, and what they NEED. In a short time, you'll be a leading voice in Westminster, strong, trusted, and honest. And then quite possibly, a move to 10 Downing Street."

She looked at me with those warm, passionate eyes. "I could do wonders with the décor in that drab place."

Morgan dead, Merle ... And Gwen wanting to get back together?

"Isn't it time to go home, Art? All the years passed like pebbles swept toward the sea by a babbling brook ... I made mistakes. I did what I did as a selfish girl captivated by her draw on men, and I shoved a dagger in your heart." Tears again, like morning dew on her cheeks. "I don't deserve forgiveness. But I'll ask you for it anyway."

Strong. Intelligent. Passionate. That's my wife, alright.

I think I'll keep her.

"Can I ask one question?"

"Of course, my love."

"When Merle was about to ... pass, did you notice him do anything, unusual?"

"Well, I *was* writhing in agony, Art. I did suffer two cracked ribs from that beatdown I took. And unusual *is*

Merle's middle name." Gwen looked pensive, then curious. "But I think that he touched his left ear, once or twice. I didn't remember that … until just now."

"Ah," I smiled. "Maybe we won't be working without a net after all."

"We?" she replied. "Does that mean I should set you up with a Twitter feed, Mr. Candidate?"

And we two friendly old lovers laughed and spent the afternoon planning our homecoming as the new world outside the window rushed by, bright and full of life.

ABOUT THE AUTHOR

Michael A. Clark has been published in *Galaxy's Edge*, *Tales from the Moonlit Path*, *Liquid Imagination*, *Mystery Weekly Magazine*, Gypsum Sound Tales anthologies *Colp* and *Thuggish Itch*, *Cosmic Horror Magazine*, the benefit anthology *Burning Love and Bleeding Hearts* and *Moonlight & Misadventure*. "Triage" appeared in November's *Etherea*. Mike lives in Charlotte, North Carolina and works in industrial automation while spending as much time as he can outdoors. He writes short stories and music because that's what he does.

YOU MIGHT ALSO ENJOY

THE ALCHEMIST DAUGHTER
by Paul S. Moore

When a concoction of ethers channels a little of their magic properties to one location, inspiration springs to life.

THE INN OF THE SEVEN STARS
by Kevin Beckett

A tale of an inn with good music, tasty food, strong beer ... and inadvertent necromancy.

WE HAVE ALWAYS LIVED IN THE BREAK ROOM
by Michael Allen Rose

Wahl'ter Dinsdale has been the master accountant for the tribe of the break-room for many seasons.

Available in digital and trade paperback editions from
Water Dragon Publishing
waterdragonpublishing.com/dragon-gems

www.ingramcontent.com/pod-product-compliance
Lightning Source LLC
Chambersburg PA
CBHW021601310726
48972CB00003B/896